For all the children of the world

*To Justin and Zoey, my children
I hope you will always live, learn and
dream, freely, in your black skin*

Copyright 2020 by Cameile Graham

ISBN: 9798672048673
All rights reserved. Beyond Color: A book that promotes love and equality for all races and skin color

No part of this book may be copied for use, in any format whatsoever, stored in a retrieval system, or transmitted in any form or by any means, electronic, mechanical, photocopying, recording, or otherwise, without permission of the author/publisher. For information regarding permission, write to camsgra@gmail.com

ISBN: 9798672048673
Printed in the United States of America
First Edition 2020

ValueReadsBooks

Beyond Color

Written by
Cameile Graham

Illustrated **by**
Onionime

A book that promotes love and equality for all races and skin color

You are me, and I am you —
beyond color.

Cameile Graham

I wanted a best friend more than anything else.
So, I asked God for a brother. To me, that made sense.
And I knew if he said yes, I'd gain a friend
and a brother who would be the best.

Well, God said yes with a brother of dark chocolate skin color.
That same day, I gained more than a best friend and a brother. I gained love like no other.

We became a happy family and I personally knew,
Malik became my brother and best friend to teach me lessons that were new.
The greatest of those lessons that I would learn,
is that love has many colors other than mine.

When I stand up for my brother, I communicate to the whole world that I am **anti-racist.**
Malik has a voice to defend himself, but when I speak up for him it means more,
sending a strong message to people of my skin color.

Being **anti-racist,** I participate in Malik's defense as long as I see any form of injustice toward my brother. I contribute by **doing** instead of only saying I believe in love and equality for all people of all races and skin color.

As brothers, we lived, learned, played and grew closer. As best friends, we often pursued many forbidden adventures, getting in and out of trouble, together. We fell in love — humans beyond color.

As we became closer, I grew more curious about Malik and where he came from.

I'd come to realize that I knew very little about the history of different races and their journey.

So, I asked Stepmom Merna to teach me more about her, and my best friend and brother.

Instead, we open doors to love, equality and respect. The more we learn about each other, the more we find out what God intended for us why we met.
I am Malik and he is me, regardless of color.

As I became more educated about races, and the background of Malik and people of color, I sincerely thanked God for his sense of humor. I could see that Malik and I were more alike than we were different because of our skin color.

The outside world constantly tries to influence us to question the love what we have found together. Somehow, by the world system that exists, we are supposed to see our skin color as a dividing factor. We have both proudly rejected that idea.

Sometimes, my friends reject Malik for standing out in his bold chocolate skin among us.
It often frustrates me to see my brother saddened because others who look like me are ignorant, hence racist.

We are growing in a family that teaches us to celebrate each other as equals.
Neither Malik's skin color nor mine gives us any greater nor lesser entitlements.
Our parents show us this example between them every day.
We admire and follow that way.

When we disagree about this and that as brothers,
we never insult each other's skin color.
Our parents reward us equally for our successes,
and deny us the same opportunities of no honor.

Mom and Dad provide us with the same access to quality formal education.
Together, we learn to be boys who have no limits growing into the best men.
Because we see beyond color, we are positioned to be the best of ourselves for tomorrow.

When God granted me my wish for a best friend in a brother,
I gained true love and the understanding that love knows no race or color.

I use to wish for a best friend and a brother that looked just like me.
Instead, God gave me a best friend and a brother that looks like true love.
Together, our love has started a change in the world.

Beyond

EQU
HUMA
UNDER
EDUC
L

Color

Made in the USA
Middletown, DE
12 September 2020